p55, p58.

SMR Focus final

65-76

98-105

9/08

SITT
MARIE ROSE

By The Same Author

MOONSHOTS (poetry) Beirut 1966.

FIVE SENSES FOR ONE DEATH (poetry) The Smith,
   New York 1971.

JEBU suivi de L'EXPRESS BEYROUTH-ENFER (poetry)
   P.J. Oswald, Paris 1973.

PABLO NERUDA IS A BANANA TREE (poetry) Da Almeida,
   Lisbon 1982.

FROM A TO Z (poetry) The Post-Apollo Press, Sausalito 1982.

THE INDIAN NEVER HAD A HORSE & OTHER POEMS (poetry)
   The Post-Apollo Press, Sausalito 1985.

JOURNEY TO MOUNT TAMALPAIS (essay) The Post-Apollo
   Press, Sausalito 1986.

THE ARAB APOCALYPSE (poetry) The Post-Apollo Press,
   Sausalito 1989.

THE SPRING FLOWERS OWN & THE MANIFESTATIONS OF THE
VOYAGE (poetry) The Post-Apollo Press, Sausalito, 1990

© Des Femmes Paris 1978
© The Post-Apollo Press for U.S. Edition 1982
Library of Congress Catalog Number 82-062030
Cover and book design by Simone Fattal

Third edition 1992.   ISBN 0-942996-18-6
Printed in the U.S.A. on acid-free paper.

Etel ADNAN

SITT
MARIE ROSE

A NOVEL

Translated from the French by Georgina Kleege

THE POST-APOLLO PRESS

POST-APOLLO PRESS
35 Marie Street, Sausalito, California 94965

TIME I

A MILLION BIRDS

NOV   1994

He must think highly of her intelligence

Marie Rose ~ p. 24

1-24

Mounir is on the phone. He is planning to make a film and wants me to write the scenario. He wants it to be about a young Syrian worker that his friends and he would convince, while on a hunting trip, to come to Lebanon.

The next night Mounir shows a super-8 color film he shot in the Syrian desert and in South-East Turkey.

The film appears on the screen. I see open expanses in the dust and wind. There is the color of swirling dust, and vast skies streaked with red fire. Then there is the Volkswagen jeep, driven by Pierre, with Mounir, Tony, and Fouad inside. The hunting rifles are clearly in view.

IMAGES BOOST

We turn to a shot of birds crossing the sky in airplane formations. Images from 1944 newsreels or from the war films which used them. The terrain is like Libya's, and the hunters resemble the sunburned soldiers of the Afrika Korps.

There are some beautiful shots: a marsh the jeep crosses with great splashes. The mud has an ochre color which sat-

Mounir attempts to exploit everyone for his "artistic" endeavors. He is unethical.

isfies. The birds return but it is darker now. The sunset is marvelously intense. The hunters aim their rifles toward the sky like missile launchers. They laugh. They show their teeth, their vigor, their pleasure.

Mounir comments in a loud voice. His wife, two sisters-in-law and one of their friends are seated on the floor. He has an audience of women in one of Beirut's most beautiful houses. One of the girls present is Tony's cousin, and she takes it all with a rather spiteful air. The "men" refused to take her hunting in Turkey. They didn't want to be bothered.

Suddenly, we hear a Pink Floyd song. Staccato. To the rhythm of this staccato music birds fall. The synchronization is perfect. Tony shoots. A bird falls. Pierre shoots. A bird falls. Mounir shoots. A bird falls. Fouad shoots. A bird falls. All their faces glow. Except Fouad's. Fouad is the perfect killer. He suffers from never having killed enough. The bullet in the body of the bird sinks into something soft. It lacks that hard, dry, satisfying contact.

Fouad hunts as though obsessed. He prefers killing to kissing. He hates the expression "to make love" because you don't make anything, as he says. He prefers jeep-speed-desert-bird-bullet to girl-in-a-bed-and-fuck. Even orgies bore him because he finds no sport in being shut in with a bunch of people, getting high on hashish. He is always disgusted by promiscuity.

Mounir, Tony, and Pierre like to do a little of everything. They dabble. Mounir's family is extremely rich, and he includes Tony and Pierre in his projects and distractions. Fouad is a part of the "group." None of them has ever found in a woman the same sensation of power he gets from a car. An auto rally is more significant than a conjugal night, and hunting is better still. There's a hierarchy even in the world of sport. In any case, hunting remains the most noble occupation. It's more wholesome. It's also more intellectual. One leaves Lebanon, and comes to know the neighboring (and enemy) country of Syria. The Syrians are not as rich and well-equipped, and lack the proper style . . . to hunt as well. Before, it was the Europeans with faces like the ones we saw on the screen, who went hunting in Syria and Iraq, and elsewhere. Now it's the Christian, modernized Lebanese who go wherever they like with their touristo-military gear. They bring their cameras to film their exploits, their puttees, their shoes, their shorts, their buttons and zippers, their open shirts and their black hair showing. And these four are particularly pure. They never sleep together. (Homoerotic)

The film ends with an image of the car filled with the bird feathers that cover the perforated, sagging bodies. In hunting like this, the Volkswagen has replaced the dog, serving all its functions.

Mounir explains with a certain modesty, that he had problems with his film. Everyone reassures him. It's fine like that. It's a little masterpiece in any case. Those birds flying in formation, what truth in Nature! It all holds together!

"You didn't see anything, really," Mounir says, "I can't

3

tell you what the desert is. You have to see it. Only, you women, you'll never see it. You have to strike out on your own, find your own trail with nothing but a map and a compass to really see it. You, you'll never be able to do that."

It's true. "We women" were happy with this little bit of imperfect, colored cinema, which gave, for twenty minutes, a kind of additional prestige to these men we see every day. In this restrictive circle, the magic these males exert is once again reinforced. Everybody plays at this game.

"Next time, you'll take us with you," one of us says without really believing it. The others don't even bother to answer.

Mounir calls me back on the phone a few days later. "You know, I have an idea. I have to see you. I want to make a film with you. But it will be my film. I just want to make it with you."

In one of the rooms of Mounir's wife's big house we hold our first meeting about the film.

"I'm going to tell you right away what I want. You know how much the cinema interests me. But I can't give up my business affairs to devote myself completely to it. Still, I want to make a commercial film, a real film, even if it takes me ten years. I want to prove to myself that I can do it.

"And then there are my scruples. You know how much I love Syria. And I know Syria. I go to all the out-of-the-way places. I go all over.

"You take a Syrian village—which makes me think I

4

should take you there."

"I know about Syrian villages. I often spent summers there as a child."

"A village off the main roads. One of those villages with the houses whose roofs are shaped like sugar loaves, cones and cubes, with everything made of earth, everything golden in the sun. The people there are very simple, very hospitable, not at all ruined."

"What? Don't they have radio?"

"Yes. But when we arrived, we were the first Europeans they had ever seen. Excuse me, I mean Lebanese."

Yes, I know. The first modernized people."

"That's right. You see, before it was foreigners, now it's we who represent all that's modern. They looked at our equipment, our rifles . . ."

"You mean your machine guns, don't you?"

"That's right. The power of our guns was unimaginable to them."

"You killed a lot of birds?"

"No. There are more birds there than in Lebanon, but you'd have to say Syria has already lost the wildlife it had. Our next trip will be to Turkey. It's still virgin for hunters there. There's everything anyone could want."

All right, having arrived in this village, what's your idea for the film?"

"You see, they're astonished. They admire us. I make friends with them. And then I go back more than once to this Syrian village. Each time they recognize us, and each time they have changed. They are not the same since they have seen us."

"And then what?"

"I want to bring one or two of them back to Beirut. I want to invite them to come.

"You'll bring them back, or will they come on their own?"

"I don't know yet, but it doesn't matter. You see, a young Syrian in Beirut, it's like us in Paris."

"You mean a Syrian from one of those villages?"

"Of course."

"I see. You want to make a film like those that show the Algerian workers in Paris."

"That's right. But I'm not sure. First, there's the beauty of the desert I want to describe. You don't know what it's like."

"Yes, but a film that's too esthetic won't play."

"Too esthetic, no. But for me, if I'm going to make this film, since money is no problem, I want to make it from the point of view of the hunters. They're proud of their superiority, but they love this village. It's so pretty, so innocent."

"The thing that interests me is the Syrian in Beirut."

"Of course. And it won't be just one, but two or three. That way, each will have his own story."

"In that case, find me two or three construction sites where you know the contractor, and where I can go to familiarize myself with the life of Syrian workers in Lebanon. There must be two hundred thousand here now."

"But they've already adapted to life in Beirut. Nothing surprises them anymore."

"It remains to be seen that nothing surprises them. In any case, I've heard a lot about them. I need to familiarize myself with them, their special problems, the atmosphere . . ."

"No, no. You don't understand. You'll write the script. I'll make the film."

"I can't write a script from nothing."

"For the moment, I'll take you to Syria . . ."

"But it's what happens here that counts."

"That's your point of view, not mine."

"This film should say something. These people have problems, their own lives. There's something very important to be said."

"Let me do it. I've thought of bringing my friend Jean-Pierre from Paris. He knows Lebanon and makes films."

"Find a director here, in Beirut, from the young ones who are just coming back from abroad."

"Either they'll steal my idea, or will want to do it their own way. I want someone who will help me do what I want. This contrast . . ."

"In that case, get your friend to come."

*

Jean-Pierre has done some video and photography. He's a bit lost before Mounir's nervous tension. He agrees with me that the red skies of the desert would not make a suitable subject for a feature-length film, especially since Mounir wants to show it in festivals, and in commercial theatres. He proposes that we take two Syrian workers already living and working in Beirut, and that the film ends with the integration of one relaxing in the pleasure-seeking society of Hamra Street (pinball included), while the other comes to a bad end. "He kills his foreman," I say. Jean-Pierre pouts. Mounir gets angry. "You're already at the end of your story," he says, "while I want to show how happy they are in those Syrian villages, what wisdom they had there, how integrated they are with Nature."

"Spring in Syria," Jean-Pierre says, "is something marvelous. I know."

"Listen, Mounir," I say, "Explain your idea and we'll go to work on it. In the meantime, I'll make a tour of a building site. I've always wanted to see one up close. Now I'll have an excuse."

*

In The City, this center of all prostitutions, there is a lot of money and a lot of construction that will never be finished. Cement has mixed with the earth, and little by little has smothered most of the trees. If not all. From every window what we call this city appears like a huge game of colored blocks consumed by the sun. You have to rise very early in the morning, before dawn really, to see how the light which comes from behind Mount Sannine transfigures the landscape. Then, among all these volumes of pale translucide colors, no foreign form, neither tree nor open spaces, comes to break the rhythm. These volumes form a gigantic pile of building blocks, which gives me, each time I see it, a sensation of almost mystic terror, like a feeling I had one dawn in the indian pueblo at Taos.

But after an hour a mean gray falls on this half-commercial, half-industrial city, and contrasts are affirmed: luxury apartment buildings next to hovels. Apartment buildings grow, concrete cages mounted patiently one on top of the other.

On the street where I live there are several big buildings under construction that will take two full years to complete. In the quarter there are others. It is a largely Christian quarter in this city where the ghetto instinct that characterized the old Middle East is still active. One could even say that Beirut is divided by a line running from north to south, with the essentially Moslem quarters to the west, and the Christian quarters to the east, while here and there, especially along the waterfront, there is a sort of no-man's-land of tourism and prostitution.

In the construction sites Mounir recommended I chat with Syrian workers. They are for the most part young, simple, unskilled, cement workers, mostly seasonal. It's like it is everywhere: cheap labor from the host country's point of view, but considerable from the point of view of the salaries charged for it. The contractor is fierce. He talks to the workers like to subhumans, like to beasts of burden who go on two legs only because the narrowness of the stairways makes it impossible to go on four. He is necktied and suited. He arrives in superb and enormous cars, cars made obscene by the size of their trunks, Buicks and Chevrolets. The workers are small, supple, muscular, shy, furtive, and above all, silent.

I try to get them talking. They refuse. According to them, everything is always all right. At noon they sit on the ground, even in the dirt, as they did in their villages. A little cement mixes with their food. At night, they sleep on the story where they are working. There are never any toilets on these sites. Again it is on the ground that everything happens. So these sites are never without their stench. When it rains it's the same. They remain riveted to their places in the wind and the wet and wait for it to end. When an elevator is installed it is kept locked. Only the contractor, the owner, and the clients have keys. If a stone needs to be raised ten stories, it goes on foot. That's all.

I talk to them about their village. They say it's back there. Very far. Beirut is very nice. What was their first reaction to this city? God protect it, they reply. Do their families miss them? I don't know, is the response. Or else no, I send them money. Do they like the Lebanese? Of course, they say. They're our brothers. They're just more advanced. They have big cars and beautiful houses.

When I tell Mounir that there is nothing to be had here but the circles under the eyes, the bent backs, the sorrow, the infernal noise of the cement mixers, the sun that beats, and the rain that gnaws, and that it could all be said very briefly with a few big images and nothing more, he's disappointed. His film, decidedly, turns around nothing.

*

On the thirteenth of April 1975 Hatred erupts. Several hundred years of frustration re-emerge to be expressed anew. Sunday noon a bus full of Palestinians returning to their camp passes a church where the head of the Phalangist party and other Christians are celebrating the mass. That morning a Phalangist was killed in front of that church. A laid trap or simple chance, no one knows, but militiamen stop the bus, make its occupants get off, and shoot them one after the other. The news crosses the city like an electric shock. A silence falls over the whole afternoon. Everyone senses the impending doom. At night, explosions shake the city. Machine gun bursts are heard at closer and closer intervals. The Palestinians avenge their thirty dead. The Phalangists counterattack.

All the quarrels of the Arab world have their representatives here. They all participate in the carnage. The wretched and the down-trodden are terrorized. It is the carnage of the new grass; a body seems to fall every second.

Monday morning there is a gathering of people around a Mercedes. The driver received several bullets in the head. His brains stick to the interior walls; matter adheres to matter.

Many factions participate in the general terrorism, but the principal protagonists remain the Christian right and the Palestinian refugee-militants, that the former seems to want to eliminate entirely.

Very rapidly the combat takes on the aspect of a civil war, and one that will last. The April air is perfumed and warmth mixes with freshness. The artillery booms. The local militia has greater fire power than the regular army.

This evening the sky is streaked with huge flashes of lightning that break it up from end to end. The streets I can see from my ninth floor are empty as in the work of a primitive painter. The song of a muezzin drifts from far away to this Christian quarter of Achrafieh, and has something unearthly about it, even if one knows it is only a record. The Middle East lives its destiny. No sound seems trivial or ordinary. The power of terror is totalitarian. Bullets crack and resonate in the amphitheatre that is Beirut. The location is perfect. The sound of the guns is echoed off the great stretched surface of the sea. Thunder mixes with the rhythmic sounds of war which purge Beirut. It ceases to be a city of merchants and becomes masses of killers let loose on a cosmic background.

Violence rises from every square meter as if from a metallic forest. During these days human reason appears like an insulating body, an impotent power. The city is an electro-magnetic field into which everyone wants to plug himself. It is no longer a place of habitation, but a being which resembles a runaway train. The most elementary fear of pain prevents me from participating in this battle. Kid- nappings of passers-by and torture become daily events. Women stay at home more than ever. They consider war like an evening of scores between men. Violence is absorbed like a consumer product. I understood this need for violence one day in front of an electric wire torn from its socket. In the two holes there remained two little bits of brilliant copper wire which seemed to call out to me. And I wanted to touch them, to reunite them in my hand, to make that current pass through my body, and see what it was like to burn. I resisted only with an extraordinary effort.

The whole country is responding without reserve to this call to violence. The pleasure of killing with all the justi- fication one could find for it blooms. On the barricades, which are also called barriers, as though it were necessary both to hold back the weight of a quarter's anger as well as

[margin notes, handwritten]: Quick Adrenaline Rush, then you're dead. Patriarchial Ethnocentrists like Mounir cannot resist it.

to keep out the enemy, youths who have not even properly slept with a woman display their blood-stained shirts. Or they ride around in cars whose red splashes haven't been washed off. On the contrary.

The week passes in counting corpses. It seems that a cease-fire would be accepted by all parties. Then Saturday night, through arson or sabotage, the port burns. The heiress of the alcohol shipping company comes out onto her balcony. Her house faces the flames. The port is part of her legend. From her terrace parallel with the sea she tries to call the fire department. But the port burns until seven in the morning.

Sunday morning, for the first time in a week, I go into the street and get my car. At a red light, a little girl with blue-green eyes comes up, in the guise of begging, to sell me a little blue stone. I send her away and regret it because, for a moment, she gave to this shapeless thing called the world, a kind of life. Oh, patience of the sun!

The flag of the Viet Cong flies over Ho Chi Minh City. That's the newspaper headline. It's the first of May, and the explosions during the night show that "it will continue." Immediately, all circulation stops. Everyone feels a prison closing in, and keeps making a lot of phone calls. Space shrinks. From balconies and terraces, people count the shots fired, their variety and intensity. All day we listen to foreign radio stations to know what's going on. Here there is neither government nor news.

They fight in the moonlight. At night sounds are more distinct. Rockets are launched from the Slaughterhouse on Dekouaneh, others fall from Mkalles on Tell Zaatar, the Palestinian camp. The artillery booms. With a straight line, Death strikes out the horizon.

From midnight until four o'clock there are cars on the street, but they are less numerous. They belong to the Phalangist militia. My apartment has picture windows and is in the middle of an open space, so I can use it as an observatory. The mountains are illuminated. Electricity shines there close to the stars. The detonations are staccato, dry. Mortars smash like so many rotten melons, and houses fall with a soft sound. Rockets whip against buildings and dynamite explodes like an evil eye. Then there is the machinegun fire, the coded messages of a victorious will. To mark the victory of Death, the city burrows deeper into terror. Soon the city will be nothing but a wrecked shell thrown up on its rocks.

The city is more deserted than if there were a curfew. You can no longer see the snipers. Bullets seem to leave by themselves. There are more than two hundred ships in the port waiting to unload their merchandise, and since they are all lit at night, Beirut appears to have moved over the sea. Minutes seem to have fewer than sixty seconds. They go faster. The mechanism of time is out of order.

The hastily established military government announces the "news." What they broadcast, however, aren't war reports, but reports of sadism. Every hour the radio reports blindings, castrations, nylon bags full of cut-up bodies thrown onto public squares, deaths by kitchen knives, a disturbing surgery, torture in a cemetery.

Mounir and his friends are at my house. Pierre is financing the Phalangists who defend, he says, the Lebanese Right and business. Tony doesn't belong to the party, neither does he, but he "supports" it. He is solicited by his friends who are already recruited. He encourages them to fight, comforts them, serves as a liaison agent. He has friends all over and reports news from the adversary camp.

"The Palestinians are very demoralized," he says. "In the camps they sleep in shelters right by the open gutters. They've lost a thousand men."

"That's nothing," Fouad says, "to what they have coming. We've only lost a hundred and fifty. That's all. The rest were all civilians—so many lost bullets. As soon as there's a lull, we'll install more guns on other points of the hill. They'll get it from all sides."

They drink. They eat. They go away. The concierge of the building comes up. He has only one hand, having lost the other in a work accident. That doesn't prevent him from having a Kalachnikov. He's haggard. "They're shooting from the building next door." I say they're not. There's no one but Syrian workers in the building next door, and they've been hiding behind their cement walls for days.

I go out on the balcony. Out in the night, in single file, their arms raised above their heads in surrender, the Syrian

16

workers are rounded up by the militia and brought to the Party Interrogation Center. I call up the businessman who lives across the street and is a friend of mine, "Look what they're doing to those workers. Tell those militia men to leave them alone. They're innocent. They'll listen to you." But this man who owes all his money to the Arabs of the Gulf, hates the Arabs, and above all, wants no trouble. He hides under his bed.

I tell myself that it would be better to let loose a million birds in the sky over Lebanon, so that these hunters could practice on them, and this carnage could be avoided.

*

An obscure story of Iraqis invited to a political discussion by the Christian militia sparks new fighting. It is already the third reprise of combat and it seems like the infernal circle will never cease turning.

From my terrace, I see the young couple who live downstairs making love on their verandah in the middle of the afternoon. Recent events must have stunned them. They never would have been so innocent normally. Maybe they're trying to overcome their anxiety. For me, time is dead. Action is fragmented into sections so that no one has an exact image of the whole process. The imagination of those holed up at home cannot travel even as far as the nearest bombings. It too halts before the police barricades.

My spine is like a twisted, stunted, fallen tree, disappearing in the sun. Attentively, I go through the morning paper. On its reduced pages, are presented regularly, little paragraph after little paragraph, the atrocities of the day. The air is full of cycles of terror which succeed each other with unbelievable speed. Crime's diversity bursts into broad daylight. When the adversary camp, the Palestinians or the Left, strikes a blow, the reprisal is immediate: they fire on the Moslem neighborhoods or on the camps, or else they arbitrarily arrest Syrian workers, on the street if possible or in the building sites, and massacre them. Then these are taken to the morgue in packages of twenty or thirty. When they beat up one by himself, they leave him on the street to be quickly removed, so that no epidemic will start up in these little streets which are less and less spared from shooting.

Saturation and panic begin to make themselves felt. Phone calls between friends become shorter and more frequent. In the street younger and younger militia men make their appearance. They employ children for their suppleness. They crawl under the line of fire and gather up abandoned arms in the adversary camp. They also learn to love the Party and how to die.

The hospitals are full. As soon as there is a calm that lasts for more than an hour, one ventures out to a hospital to visit the wounded. There are many amputees. The cases without hope wait in the hall.

My eyes are like plants that open during the day and close at night. I begin to wish that two rockets would pass through my head leaving me intact . . . that's what it means. Everything becomes primitive. The cells remember the solar pulses of their first days, back when they were still sleeping, back in the prehuman stage. Everything that has been learned seems to become blurred. Bodies, too, erupt like hatred, like lemons squeezed to the point of bursting.

The radio announces that due to public pressure there is once again a new government. Still, no one dares to venture into the street. The explosions have diminished. The intervals of silence are trying, though, because the wait for the next event becomes unbearable. In a way, the explosions provided a necessary release. One can't tell anymore.

Wednesday morning, after a relatively quiet night, people tentatively go out. An odor of hot decay grabs at the throat. It's the second of July and the sun strikes hard and all over. The sun wearies those who have been hiding inside. The trash cans form mountains on which the children of this parkless and gardenless city play, both rich and poor. The trash cans have replaced people on the streets. They are numerous, viscous, and omnipresent. It's hot and windy. Many stores are gutted or destroyed. Powdered glass is the only thing that seems clean in this filth; it glitters on the asphalt of the streets.

19

At the Café Express a few people talk. A.N. tells me that the Arabs, also, don't understand hatred of the enemy. They only hate among themselves. They are still in that primitive stage where only family quarrels interest them, intimate battles, fratricide. They are only preoccupied with themselves. That's how he explains the fierceness of this civil fight which isn't even a war.

Street after street I cross the city. Beirut is humiliated. She suffered the defeat; she's the one who lost. She's like a dog with her tail between her legs. She was heedless to the point of folly. She gathered the manners and customs, the flaws and vengeance, the guilt and debauchery of the whole world into her own belly. Now she has thrown it all up, and that vomit fills all her spaces. In the Christian quarters, fierce and puritanical, arrogance flies its flag at half mast. The expressions on faces are hard. The young people with their khaki clothes, those who carry rifles, those who ride in jeeps without license plates, those who still have hoods, those who display revolutionary folklore without realizing the contradiction, those who spit on every car that passes, those who sell the Phalangist newspaper, all of them wear faces of false victory.

The Moslem quarters are more disordered, more colorful. The trash cans here are bigger and more evident. There is less bravado in the eyes and more sorrowful resignation. There is no panic left except for a crease around the mouth. The remains of barricades are more apparent, more improvised, and a certain nonchalance leaves its impact on gestures, faces, and the atmosphere.

More westernized and efficient in war as in everything, the Christian quarters have a sort of austerity which links them to certain "*pieds-noirs*" neighborhoods in Nice and Marseille, or to little towns in Sicily and Greece. The Moslem enclaves still retain the disorder of the Orient which is still the last good in these essentially bastard countries which have no precise culture except for the one that developed from a pell-mell of values in a state of disintegration. You would have to seek out someone squatting in a corner, someone not yet fanaticized by the tornado in order to touch some semblance of humanity, which, like a compass, still marks the magnetic North of the human species.

But who actually lost besides the inhabitants of this city and a few animals people forgot to feed or were also killed under the rain of bullets? Horses burned in their stables at the Hippodrome. This city is like a great suffering being, too mad, too overcharged, broken now, gutted, and raped like those girls raped by thirty or forty militia men, and are now mad and in asylums because their families, Mediterranean to the end, would rather hide than cure . . . but how does one cure the memory? The city, like those girls, was raped. Here, passing me now is a Mercedes taxi, burned out and towed by another. Its black paint is charred like human flesh. It's like a human being on four instead of two legs, being dragged to the hospital, or to the morgue. It resembles all that has been.

*

It seems a relative calm has come. Thursday morning the third of July I read the newsaper. There is again, maybe the last for a long time, the now-famous daily column listing the recent "incidents." I read the eulogy for the anonymous and the known, hastily shrouded underground or in the memory, the rapid list of names and facts, such as they are,drawn up by Beirut's French language daily.

- The Christian quarters have been cleared of the armed youths who held control there. A young man, Marcel Yousef Mansour, shot by a sniper on the roof of a building in Tayoune, succumbed to his wounds at l'Hotel-Dieu. Also dead was Hamade Azzam of Sin el Fil.
- The removal of the twelve bodies abandoned on the street at the Port, in Achrafieh, and Place Debbas, proceeded normally.
- A sniper near St. Joseph's Hospital in Dora spread panic in the quarter. The police undertook to find the man in order to capture him.
- Jean Yousef Khachane, Yasine Aballah Bacha, Yousef

Farsane, Ahmed Mohammed Hijzi, Ali Hasan Ghadour, and Mohammed Ali Moussa were killed by stray bullets at Ain Remmaneh.

- Two rockets destroyed the establishment of Abdel Kader Zaatari.
- At five o'clock in the morning two mortars fell on the police station at Tarik Jedideh. Three police officers died.
- On rue Sannine the body of a man of about twenty years of age was discovered. The face had been badly mutilated. An inquest to identify the victim is now underway.
- Near the site of Tueiti on the Zahle-Dhour el Choueir Road the bodies of Antoine Yacob Moubarak (38 years old) and of Jean Elias Abou Assi (20, originally of Hadeth) were found. They were killed in Moubarak's car (Mercedes, registered 135525) and their bodies thrown in a ditch. On the same road, known to be unsafe, the body of Daoud Kharrat was also found.
- A mortar shell fell in Hammana near the public garden, killing a little girl.
- Tuesday night an unidentified person opened fire in Louayze on Michel Sacre. He was later found at the wheel of his car, shot once in the head.
- The bodies of three Syrian workers were found in the room they occupied in Dekouaneh.

*

The red skies of Syria parade before my eyes. It's impossible to go on reading . . . this reading I've done every day for a month.

This morning I telephoned Mounir. "You saw the paper?" I asked him. He says, "Yes. Why?"

"You know, those three Syrian workers that were found in their room in Dekouaneh, with bullets in their heads, you know?"

"Yes. Why?"

"You don't think, when you make your film, that we could finish it like that: the three Syrian workers that you bring back from their village die in this room. There have been more than two hundred killed like that."

"No. I would never be able to show my film in Lebanon in that case. Not even in other Arab countries. And besides, no. I want my workers to have trouble in Lebanon, but not that much. It's too violent. It's too political. And anyway, to defend my point of view, I want one of them to get back to his village."

"I think Mounir that I really can't make this film with you."

"Don't worry about it. Tony, Fouad, Pierre and I will discuss it. I'll find someone. You come to the house for dinner tonight."

TIME II

MARIE-ROSE

I

1.

In this classroom, always occupied by the air and the few flies that can survive at the height of this hill, there's US, the deaf-mutes. We're here to learn the special languages that will help us communicate with others. We read words on lips whose sounds don't reach us. We utter sounds that make people shudder it seems. We can't hear them. We can use our fingers for an alphabet. But above all else, we can dance. Pressed against radios, our hands recognize the music, and we dance like charmed snakes, the vibrations guiding us.

Because we're deaf, we can forecast earthquakes. Besides, there's one every day in Beirut. The civil war has been going on for almost a year, and they're still fighting. They started with rifles and tommy-guns, now they blast each other with 155 millimeter cannons. In this quarter that hangs over the city, windows shatter before our eyes.

She came this morning, Sitt Marie-Rose, followed by

29

four men. What beautiful guns they have! We children said
to ourselves that this class would not be as normal. Something's going on. Normally the soldiers don't come into the
school. They're everywhere else, in the street, on the roofs,
in the shops. Today, here they are. They're sitting up on the
platform where she usually sits. She stands before us. She's
beautiful. For an Arab, it's rare, she has blue eyes. She has
children of her own. Three of them. But they go to school
somewhere else, not here. They're not deaf-mutes. We feel
a strange calm. They've told us that there's a truce. There's
one every five days. It won't last. The air isn't moving at all.
It's February. The weather's cold and damp. Today, the
sky's blue. Nothing happens. Why did they come? She looks
unhappy. But there's a truce. They told us. She doesn't like
the war. Neither do we, because we can't take part in it.

2.

Why did I come up? I'm the director of this school and I teach here. I had to pay the teachers, and to find myself among these children again. My own are on the other side of the city. These are so vulnerable. They can't hear the guns, but it's worse for them because they can feel them. They jump. They know their space is violated ceaselessly. They know that buildings fall. They walk over the debris. They know that people are dying. They're doubly walled in, by the events that have closed their country on itself, and by their own double handicap.

I know, everyone warned me not to cross the line which divides the city into two enemy camps, to come back to this Christian zone where I've always lived. But there was a cease-fire, and normally they never bother women. And the longer it lasts, the more one relaxes one's vigilance, so I told myself that there was no more danger coming here, than there would have been, in normal times, crossing the

Marie "crosses lines"
tribal
ethnic
christian/refugee camp etc

31

women aren't
significant but
Marie becomes
significant in
men's life

street. There died pedestrians in Beirut as many as would flies before what we call nowadays "the events." Cars were the precedents of those murdering weapons. They were driven with the same unpitying exasperation.

I was imprudent; I admit it. And my life depends on prudence. I knew that on both sides they've been indulging in abductions, in this battle where courage and cowardice both border and mix together in the same combatants. I myself was a horrified witness to one of those kidnappings in West Beirut, one of those perfidious dragnets, like the tongue of a huge, many-shaped millipede, and in those nets unarmed men struggled like fish torn from the sea. I didn't know then, I was far from having any idea, that I too would find myself caught in the same net, thrashing with the same impotence. But they took me, a few meters from this school, on this street where everyone always seemed to like me, before the eyes of the parents of these children who sit before me now, their eyes open, sending me signs. Nothing moved in the street except my captors. Everything seemed staged including the short flight of a bee from one tree to another. They said: "We've got to talk to you." And I understood that, with those words, I was leaving the world of ordinary speech.

Kidnapped

3.

[handwritten marginalia: mummy, Mourir, 33-45]

I had nothing to do with this abduction. In principle, I'm against any procedure that's not strictly military. I told them, at the Party's Direction, not to pursue this method. We will get our enemies. This town has no escape route. It is a one-way city. On one side there's the sea, and we control the east. We will advance westward with a vast circular movement. We'll empty the pockets of habitation, one after the other. Then we'll bomb the airport south of the city, and the circle will be closed. After three days of intensive bombardment, they'll all be taken: imprudent friends living on the other side, enemies, self-proclaimed neutrals, all of them. It will be clean and definitive. There will be a victor and a vanquished, and we'll be able to talk, to reconstruct the country from a new base. But taking prisoners, like that, haphazardly, it's pointless.

I'm their friend, it's true, but I'm also their section chief. I can't say no to my comrades. They told me: here's

[handwritten marginalia, left margin: Ethnic cleansing / break up of State]

[handwritten marginalia, right margin: Extreme individualism]

[handwritten marginalia, bottom: tribalism]

33

some really special loot, a particularly bad sort we're bringing you. You want to see?

I saw. I saw Marie-Rose. I expected to find her beaten, maybe disfigured, terrorized. No. She stands before me as beautiful as she was long ago when we were both sixteen and going to high school in Beirut. She's thirty-two now, and carries herself like a queen. I swear she is beautiful. She lived on the same street where I still live. She got married. So did I. She got divorced after having three children. I got divorced before having any. I haven't forgotten the day I held her hand for the first time at the front gate of my parents' garden. We were laughing, you don't look like an Arab, I told her, neither do you, she said. I believed she was worthy of me because she had blue eyes. You look like girls in the movies, I told her, you're so modern. She looked into my eyes and said, you're the most handsome boy in the whole school. Before the moment I met her by the drinking fountain in the school yard and she threw a few drops of water in my face, I loved nothing but my bicycle. After that I loved her face. I used to wait for her every day after school to walk a few steps behind her to her door so that the neighborhood wouldn't know that we were in love. It went on for two years including the summers which we spent in the same village. I only once left a kiss in her hair. I never forgot it. I wonder if she did.

My love for her has grown dim, but she is no stranger to me. I know her, and knowing is an extraordinarily strong bond. It establishes a kind of magnetic field between beings or even things, and intensifies and illuminates everything. She's here before me. She's familiar to me. And yet it's up to me to decide whether she lives or dies. How can I?

But since I must decide, there are things that must be known. What series of roads, of stages, of turning-points led her to this situation? I read her name in the newspapers, and saw her on television, following her various causes. First it was educational reform, then it was the typographers strike, then women's liberation.

I found it all ridiculous. I'm no longer so sure about it. Things have evolved in this country. Yes, it's taken nearly a year of civil war, hundreds dead every day in Beirut, and an upsetting of the old alliance between heaven and earth, for me to conceive of a woman as a worthy partner, ally or enemy. But I am one of the few that would admit it.

35

Tony

4.

Mounir and this woman look at each other without hatred. I don't understand. She's a Christian and she went over to the Moslem camp. She's Lebanese and she went over to the Palestinian camp. Where's the problem? We must do away with her like with every other enemy.

My name is Tony and it will never be Mohammed. It is as clear and inevitable as the succession of the hours. And no matter what anyone says, the will of the group rules. We are the Christian Youth and our militia is at war with the Palestinians. They are Moslems. So we are at war with Islam, especially when it crosses our path. If we were a flock of vultures against a flock of eagles, it would be the same thing. And in this war, there are no prisoners. There's nothing to be taken. That's how it is. We must suppress them. This woman is nothing but a bitch. Mounir should not regard her as an ordinary person.

shouldn't regard her as equal enemy sexist

IDIOT
Blind tribalist

Fouad

- killer
- n.hilist

5.   Chaos

I didn't position artillery on the hills of this city to get
myself mixed up in some story about a woman. I did it to
blow up things. A militia is a government without a governed.
A militia is always right. In all its decisions. They said to me,
you Fouad, you're an anarchist. You blow up buildings. You
gut an entire quarter like it was a watermelon. But me, I say
to them, I am absolute order. I am absolute power. I am
absolute efficiency. I've reduced all truths to a formula of
life and death.

- cant deal w/ change
- Electric charge from violence (Sade minus sex)
- fundamentalist
- sees in black and white cant
  deal w/ ambiguity

37

6.

I wonder why they wanted me to attend this indict-
ment, me who's nothing but a friar and a peasant. And then,
what did this woman do?

"Marie-Rose, do you go to mass?
"No."
"You're not a communist?"
"No."
"Then why did they arrest you?"
"Because I belong to the Palestinian Resistance."

7.

We have become strangers to each other. We're closed systems. I saw a plant and it seemed very straight to me, and to know where it was going. I allowed myself to say: I'm like that, I climb, I raise myself. I hover above this city, this country, and the continent to which they belong. I never lose sight of them. I have devoted myself to observing them up close. I identify with its geology. I've surveyed the currents which cross this part of the world, following some, opposing others, dismantling the mechanism of false alliances, and smelling out traitors like garlic in cooking. I know what's going on. But in fact, I am more like a four-footed animal than the plant. I go along with my head always to the ground.

I know the Chabab mafia, that gang of boys. They have a constant need to find themselves alone. They live in function of their vanity. They are bound together as if with steel. They parade like wild peacocks. I know the priests, the ulemas, the self-proclaimed heroes, the scholars, the women. It's essentially a monotonous and tiresome world. And yet I don't leave it. I remain among them because I want to know. Their ideas? Oh no. They'd amount to nothing but a smoky whirlwind. It's their flesh that interests. There are milleniums inside their bodies that should be exposed to daylight or examined under a microscope. There are superimposed layers of memory crammed in their brains as their dead cities are crammed under the hills. This civil war is a laser which has hit the center of their identities. It's a nuclear explosion, not from a bomb, not from the exterior, but from the very heart of their race's memory. The nearer they are to the paroxysm of violence, the more they become themselves. While living in this city which possesses all the traps of a sedentary life, they've managed to stay nomads. They love destruction because it's a process of peeling away. It makes them believe they're on the road to truth. Everything which blocks the horizon encumbers them. Even the trees. They kill them so they can see further, that is, see nothing. They use their bodies like weapons made of iron.

They love noise, they love turmoil. They don't give themselves over to thought or other long-term distractions. All they do is run headlong into death.

Pain also encumbers them. Somebody else's pain, of course; that will never touch them. Their pity, when it exists, is tribal. That's why I doubt Marie-Rose will leave this confrontation alive.

II.

oxymoron

sedentary / nomadic

not going
nowhere

movement

Circular
movement

1.

Today is no ordinary school day. Sitt Marie-Rose is sitting before these three men who have guns that are bigger than rifles. They're beautiful guns. Powerful. We're too little to use them. But there are some former students who, even though they're deaf-mutes, are in the fighting. They put them on barrages, behind big sand bags, and they defend the streets. They shoot. They see bodies fall in silence. It's like when we dream. There's no noise in this world. That's why the war doesn't stop. Nobody wants to stop it. Far away, the big powers are too busy, and besides, they never think about us. So we just keep it up. In silence. From the Gulf to the Atlantic, on our geography maps, the Arabs are all silent. The militia men think that there's nothing out there but a big desert. It must be true, otherwise people would have come to tell the people who are fighting that they shouldn't, that the streets are stained with blood like the floor of the butcher's shop. Every Sunday in the mountains

43

they cut off a sheep's head, right on the sidewalk, and take out its entrails and, later, eat its liver. It makes a little dirty stream in the street. Now they do the same thing with the Moslems and Palestinians. They say the Moslems and Palestinians do the same thing to Christians. It's possible. We are too little to cut off a sheep's head, but two years ago we learned how to cut off chickens' heads. The chickens jumped around and it was really messy. We were covered with feathers and got blood in our mouths. Sitt Marie-Rose came in and didn't want us to fool with chickens anymore. Though it is useful to know how to cut off a chicken's head. But they took away our razors and won't give them back anymore.

Nobody loves us. Our parents beat us. It makes them angry that we're deaf-mutes. They say we're worthless. We keep our sisters from making a good match. So they put us in this school and only Sitt Marie-Rose loves us. We know it because she's so patient. She doesn't rush out at the end of class like the other teachers do. She lets us come to her office when we have an argument, and she never beats us.

Twice a year she takes us to the movies. Last time we saw "The Sparrow," an Egyptian film. The people in the film were different. They were smiling and laughing all the time. They seemed happy. They didn't seem like the people in our neighborhood lately. We have been told that to be The People is to be like in the film, lots and lots of smiling folks. When we grow up, we'll be The People too. And it's not only because we're poor. We're not all poor. It's not enough just to be poor to be The People. You have to be docile and innocent. You have to be a part of things like clouds are a part of the sky.)

Today, Sitt Marie-Rose is not happy. Her eyes are dark like a valley on a summer's evening. They made her sit down before them and now they're talking to her. They're as hard as statues. They told us that we couldn't go out. Are they being punished? They must have done something really bad for her to look at them so severely. She looks like the Blessed Virgin at church, the big one, the one that stares at us during mass. She's very scary when she gets mad. But we love her. We're not scared. And she loves us. It's like the horizon on the sea.

parteial understanding
- Sael

2.

I have no illusions. I'm caught in their trap and now here they are with all the indecency of armed men before someone who's not. They hold absolute power that's as cold as their guns. I'd rather talk to their tommy-guns; they'd be less repugnant to me.

I would have to meet Mounir again, here, like this. Young, he was already worldly. He was afraid of being taken for a weakling. He had an obsessive fear of failure. He believed that he saw in others strengths that they didn't actually possess, and this vision drove him crazy. He was, however, extremely sensitive. He loved music, and had all sorts of charming quirks. For example, he would only listen to music from the garden. He moved the record player close to the window, and would listen to Chopin Etudes standing under a tree with a fine rain falling. I made fun of him, teased him. He said, you like Arab music. You like Oum Kalsoum because you like Abdel Nasser. They are alike.

He was different from his friends. He was the only one among them who loved Syria. He dreamed of going hunting there. While the others believed that unless one resembled Europeans one was nothing, he spoke of Asia as an enchanted continent, which made me think that once I had read lots and lots, I would find out which hero of History he might resemble. Asia made a halo around him, a bit like his hair. Eventually though, his friends did have an influence over him, and he too made fun of Arab cinema and everything else that belonged to the region. It was because they were taught by Jesuits who oriented them toward Paris and the quarrels of the French kings.

These young boys were exalted by the Crusades. Mounir identified with Frederick Barbarossa because he was himself slightly red-haired. He bitterly regretted, as though it had happened recently, that Saladin had conquered Jerusalem. It caused him actual pain. The Crusades excited all of them. Every year, those French priests led a procession in which all the students of the Christian schools dressed in white tunics with square red crosses sewn front and back. On their heads they wore kefieh-and-agal which made them look less like Crusaders than Arabs. They carried palm branches through the streets of Beirut singing "I am a Christian. This is my glory, my hope, my support . . ." The next day at school they were proud of having defeated the Infidels. They dreamed of a Christianity with helmets and boots, riding its horses into the clash of arms, spearing Moslem foot-soldiers like so many St. Georges with so many dragons.

Mounir left the Jesuit school to go to the French lycée. I remember telling him that, dressed up like a Crusader and marching in that procession, he must have been the most ridiculous thing in the world. He laughed and his laughter still sounds in my years: "You're just a girl. You don't know what it's like to be a twelve-year-old boy." I remember replying, "You come from here. You're not a foreigner. You don't come from France or England. You could never be a Crusader." "Are you sure?" he asked with a sadness that misted his eyes, "Then what am I going to become?"

Why does this man who is such a stranger to me now, and so hostile, make me go back so far, and reanimate these disarming images? Must I now hear again that adolescent question—"Do you smell as good as your name promises?"— which I told him was stupid, and which I never forgot? Is Death so near as to make the past surge up with such clarity that it obscures this present? And how not to get as a whip-lash the memory of that one day when, while shaking hands to say goodbye, our hands stuck together, sending a current of hot blood through our veins? They remained clasped in one another and I could no longer distinguish my fingers from his, or his breath from mine, and he put his mouth in my hair, and left running. I hung about in the street, took a walk by the seashore, and returned home about nightfall, watching the sky. I avoided speaking to my mother, avoided her eyes, pretended to be sick, and went to bed, to the cool

48

sheets, where I slept until morning on my closed fists and my tears. It was the only night of my life I slept completely dressed, like a traveler.

The children are getting restless. They want to go outside. But Fouad tells them to keep quiet and see what happens to traitors.

Me, a traitor? To whom? What did I do?

I got married at twenty. What anguish, what sadness those first years of marriage were! Everything shrank around me, even objects, even the air in my lungs. I had entered an order of boredom, in an apparent calm, in the somnolence of neighbors' visits. My armchairs began to smell like my mother's. *feminist joke* Then, I enrolled myself in the university. My husband sulked, then became angry, and finally hatred set in. He hated me violently. I continued to fight the visible and invisible things that thwarted me. I threw myself into a sort of public life, the cycle of conferences, protests, social action, planning committees, causes of all kinds. . . . My head oscillated like a planet finally free of its orbit. And then I had my children. What a wonderful thing it is to have children!

Yes. My children. My three children are waiting for me, and when they don't see me coming, they'll start to worry. They're already traumatized by the battles going on in every neighborhood. They've seen men shooting. They've seen corpses in the street and watched them intently while in the past I wouldn't even let them look at a dead rat. They

49

have breathed and still breathe the hot odor of putrified flesh, bitter-sweet and rotten, that the breeze carries from house to house. They have told me a thousand and one times the story of their friend who went swimming at the Ouzai beach, and while coming out of the water felt his ankles seized by decomposed flesh, which made him start vomiting, and run away with his folded clothes in his hand. They know that people shoot at ambulances and kill firemen. They hear their elders telling them how to tear out guts and eyes. They hear about Christians being pulled off barricades, castrated, hacked up with axes, and thrown into garbage cans. People have broken into offices to take the Moslems sitting there, draw and quarter them, and watch them die in a howl of pain. I have trouble convincing my children that all this is obscene. They think of one thing only: growing up and fighting. And when I tell them all this is absolute evil, they tell me that it's written in the Bible that God hates the enemy. And when I ask them where God is and who is the enemy, they throw themselves against my chest, kissing me, and ceasing to understand.

What did I do? After the defeat of June '67, I founded the Association of the Friends of Jerusalem. I thought that in this country where Christians hold the power, many people would feel cut off with the loss of the Holy City. But Jerusalem has no friends in this city. I thought that this feeling of frustration could be channeled into material aid for the Palestinian refugees. We were just a handful of women, putting up posters, writing letters to the newspapers that were rarely published, soliciting funds, going to foreign embassies to alert the public to the moral and material misery that reigned in the camps. They treated us like madwomen. For them, Palestine was a myth without substance. To the Palestinians as well, we were nothing but strangers at first. But we won them over. Going there was like a trip to a foreign place. Our world and theirs bordered each other, but never touched. They formed an island where thoughts of revenge grew like bamboo in the jungle. An epic was sprouting in the little streets of their camp. Their shelters, which were as damp as movie theaters, concealed arms which shone as soon as you opened the little, wooden, lockless doors. In their eyes you could read their *idées fixes*. Slogans or impatience gathered in their mouths. The cooking was done outside. By necessity it was very dull. Sometimes someone would start singing, and the song would always end with groans like those the coast makes when it's beaten by the sea. I went to the camp's insane asylum which lies between Beirut and the airport. On the ground floor, there was a window where children climbed to divert themselves. Three days ago a bomb fell near that room. That was my last visit to the camp. Three young men were keeping guard to replace the fallen wall. One of them, chilled by melancholy, said to me, "We know that we will always be able to go crazy when it becomes unbearable. But them, they're already crazy. Where can they go?"

The Crusade which I always thought was impossible has, in fact, taken place. But it's not really religious. It's part of a larger Crusade directed against the poor. They bomb the underprivileged quarters because they consider the poor to be vermin they think will eat them. They fight to block the tide of those who have lost everything, or those who never had anything, and have nothing to lose. They have turned those among them that were poor against the poor "of others." They have perverted Charity at the heart of its root. Jerusalem is the great absent. That city, founded a few thousand years ago by the Canaanites, their ancestors, where Christ died and rose—they've never been there. They don't plan to go. The spiritual Jerusalem is dead, in their consanguineous marriage, and under the weight of their hatred. It is no longer in the Middle East.

3.

Marie-Rose, you stand before me. Why did you come back to me from so far? And at such a moment? I waited several months before joining the Militia. I hesitated, but the time came when I could no longer let my comrades down. Every night they came to my house and told me that the troops knew how to fight, but they lacked a cadre of men who knew how to organize them. They were fighting from house to house, with nothing but side arms, and their extraordinary courage. Their bombardments were undirected. It hasn't been a month since I finally threw myself into the melee, and now you turn up from so long ago, to confront me with this horrible decision.

I must be dreaming. Sixteen years could not have passed since I left my first man's kiss in your hair. We were both sixteen then. I went home and to my adolescent room, that room where sports, not lover's, trophies were accumulated. A desire hotter than a Beirut August came to exas-

perate my blood, and from the successive masturbation of
that night I knew a degree of pleasure I have never attained
since. That night my mother was restless, and called to me
often: "Mounir," she said from her room, "do you want
something?" And I pushed her voice aside to be alone with
you. Now I'm afraid that the nostalgia you awaken in me
will give me a reason to despise myself, and add another
torment to my soul.

"I have some questions for you."

"What are they?"

"You have gone over to the enemy."

"What enemy?"

*psychoanalitic
she revived
a fantasy
that he supress

"The Palestinians. You are counted in the ranks of the
Palestinian Resistance. You're fighting against us."

"I worked for the social services of the Resistance long
before what you call 'the events.' And I have continued to
do so."

"Nowadays, to work for them is treason."

"I don't consider the Palestinians an enemy. They belong to the same ancestral heritage the Christian party
does. They're really our brothers." ⚹ God is Great !!

"Do you know that they yell *Allahu Akbar* at the
moment of assault?"

"And the crosses that you wear, aren't they also a sign
of allegiance to the same God, and therefore also a kind of
battle-cry?"

"Their presence in our country has been a constant

provocation."

"Because they were on vulnerable ground. Someone killed their poets while you were off hunting. Someone killed their political leaders in their sleep, while you were off driving around like wildmen on the mountain roads mimicking a Monte Carlo auto rally or the Italian Grand Prix. Someone bombed their camps while you were out dancing. People bargained with their History in the halls of the U.N., while you secretly armed yourselves with the aid of their invaders, so that one day you could stab them in the back."

"But it's our country. We're at home here."

"And since when does being at home put you above morality?"

"What morality? I only recognize the power of the State, even when that's based on nothing but violence. It's violence that accelerates the progress of a people."

"Morality is violence. An invisible violence at first. Love is a supreme violence, hidden deep in the darkness of our atoms. When a stream flows into a river, it's love and it's violence. When a cloud loses itself in the sky, it's a marriage. When the roots of a tree split open a rock it's the movement of life. When the sea rises and falls back only to rise again it's the process of History. When a man and a woman find each other in the silence of the night, it's the beginning of the end of the tribe's power, and death itself becomes a challenge to the ascendancy of the group."

"Do you really love the Palestinians?"

"I have loved these thousands of men and women who fled like rats leaving a ship invaded by stronger rats. During the years that they agreed to live in the camps where we parked them, they were treated like cowards. When they finally got themselves organized, which they had to do outside their own territory, all the Arab states were leagued to crush them, and you're going along with their decision. You think you're acting independently, but you've actually been manipulated." *can't think for yourself*

"You deny their arrogance?"

"And your own arrogance? Though, it is true you're only following the plans of the big powers to humiliate those who are already humiliated. That's not so hard."

"Marie-Rose, it's you who's being judged here, not us."

"And why not? And who would prevent me from saying what I think since this is perhaps my last opportunity?"

"It's not your last chance. We're all Christians here. It would make a difference if you'd show some regret, some doubt."

"I am the mother of three children. I left my husband. I live with a young Palestinian who is, at this moment, in danger. I was defending the Palestinian cause before I even knew him. I'm defending a common culture, a common history, theirs and ours. I don't see any difference. But if I've taken their part with pain against yours it's because our survival depends on theirs."

"I represent legality."

"They represent a new beginning. The Arab world is infinitely large in terms of space and infinitely small in its vision. It's made up of sects and sub-sects, ghettos, communities, worked by envy, rotten, closed back on themselves like worms. This world must be aired, its stiffness must be eased. For once in the History of the Middle East, the wandering of the Palestinian is no longer that of a nomad carrying his tribe in himself, but that of a man, alone, uprooted, pursued. They're attempting to break down your values, and in the process are breaking their own necks. They're getting their throats cut by you and your sinister allies. To liberate you! There are knots to untie, abscesses to drain.

"Besides things have already started to explode. It's already too late for you to crawl back to the cocoons of the past. Mixed in the blood of the dead Palestinians is as much Lebanese blood, Lebanese who died for them, and with them. For the first time in Arab History one group has died for another. You do not represent the half of the country, made up of as many Christians as Moslems, who are fighting for and with the Palestinians. I'm not the only one to do it.

"You who love victory, beware that the defeat of the Palestinians will act as leaven in the Arab psyche. You're tearing their throats out. I repeat tearing their throats out. I can hear their death-rattle. Their blood fills your mouths. But things are on the move. They are moving in Rabat,

makes a prophecy that isn't true

moving in Algiers, in Kairouan and in Tripoli of Libya, in the Fayoum and in Damascus, in Bagdad and much further ... people are arriving barefooted to claim their dues."

"And you, what are you supposed to represent?"

"I represent love, new roads, the unknown, the untried. For ten thousand years in this part of the world we've always been tribal, tribal, tribal. But Gilgamesh left alone, all ties forever broken, searching for life and death. Since that distant day we haven't invented a single man who didn't found a religion. We haven't had a single man who was effectively alone, who sought on his own account, to understand good and evil, who could stand up crucified without anyone knowing it, and carry his adventure and his secret to a grave that didn't open on either Heaven or Hell. Shepherd or sheep you always have defined yourselves in terms of herds."

get. a Christ flock

"But you're getting lost in dreams and theories. You forget their arrogance. They behaved like the masters. They walked around brandishing their arms in broad daylight. They were the ones who asserted themselves."

"Between you and them there is a misunderstanding that History will not pardon. It will lead to a cataclysm."

"This is war Marie-Rose. You can call it civil or tribal, but our comrades are dying. If tomorrow the Christian front were broken, your Palestinians would storm into our houses and there would be a massacre on the hill. Besides, I'm defending the power of the State."

"You usurped the power of the State. You're a militia."

"We represent the will of the people."

"Of part of the people. The other part—which is large—is for the Palestinians. They're fighting with them."

"First, we'll win this war. After that, we'll talk."

Liberal humanist Christian values

4. *Tony Tony*

No one is ever going to understand this ritual. Marie-Rose accuses. Mounir is accused. She shouldn't even open her mouth. He's not here to listen to her. He knows she's a criminal and that she's too pig-headed to change. It's a waste of time to try to reform a woman who takes herself seriously. She should not have had a Palestinian for a friend. She could have found someone better to sleep with. If she were my sister, I would have killed her long ago. My own sister is very nice. That's something else. She never goes out except with our mother. When you speak to her she lowers her eyes. But when whores like this get mixed up in war, now that's something to get disgusted about.

Does he sleep with his sister?

5. Fouad *Fouad*

Tony and I are getting bored. We should get it over
with. Talk, talk, talk. There's no lack of women. One less
isn't going to make a lot of difference with 30,000 dead. And
besides, we don't hold prisoners. All she had to do was not
go over to the other side. They want to be Palestinians, left-
ists, Moslems, what do I know? And what else? They're
occupying our country and she wants to help them. No
matter what country in the world you're in, a traitor is a
traitor.

And these children keep wanting to go out. Deaf and
mute they're lost from the start. But we want them to stay.
We want them to see what happens to traitors. Sitt Marie-
Rose? She conned them all right, this Sitt Marie-Rose.
They'll have to see with their own eyes what's going to
happen to her. They must learn so that later they won't get
any ideas about rebellion. You never know, nowadays, even
deaf-mutes could become subversives.

"You ate this morning, Marie-Rose?"

"Yes."

"Me, I had what I always do: raw sheep's liver with a little salt, testicles, brains—all the intimates, you know. And you had your coffee did you?"

"Yes."

"I thought as much."

"If you were a Moslem, Marie-Rose, there wouldn't have been this problem. They would have shot you at the first roadblock. But you're a Christian, and I would like it if we could still save your life."

"Save my life?"

"Yes."

"This war is a fight between two powers, two powers and two conceptions of the world. You've made it into a religious war to reinforce your ranks, to cloud the issues."

"But Islam is behind them. Therefore we are at war with Islam, whether you like it or not. They can't separate their religion from their culture, from their heritage, and neither can we. We're fighting for the road that leads to the Divine. The best road."

"How can you judge a road that you have neither laid out nor traveled on? How do you know that the desert roads lead to the Divine less well than the roads from your cities?"

"You say such things to these children? You indoctrinate them?"

"These children, as you call them, these students are deaf and mute. In this superstitious society where infirmities are viewed as the work of devils, there will never be a place for them. You'll never have to fear them. Like bats they will always be bound to obscurity."

"I'm the guardian of justice."

"When everything else is destroyed there's nothing left but love, and you don't know what that means."

"You're a Christian and you went over to the enemy. Come back to the community. You'll inhale the aromas of baking bread and of the mountains. That's a form of love. We're all brothers and sisters. It's so nice and warm."

"Bouna Lias, it's cold in the camps and I prefer it."

"Aren't you afraid of going to Hell?"

"You've already turned this country into Hell."

---

obscurity: the state of being unknown, inconspicous, or unimportant.

paganism: a religion that has many gods, goddesses, considers the earth holy, & does not have a central authority.

labyrinths: a complicated irregular network of passages or paths in which it is difficult to find one's way; a maze

saint George: slaying the dragon, rescuing the king's daughter & converting Libya is a 12th-century Italian fable. George was a favorite patron saint of crusaders as well as Eastern soldiers in earlier times. He is a patron saint of England, Germany, Aragon, Catalonia, Genoa, & Venice.

oppisation will always be met w/ violence

have no compassion?

themes
sexism
feminism
equality

capital D?

7.

omniscient

translated

The Churches of the Arab East are those of the cata-
combs, those of the Faith, of course, but also those of
obscurity. They still define themselves in opposition to an
imaginary paganism. They still haven't left the labyrinths.
They have never gotten the knife in the belly that the great
reforms were to the Church in the West. They're not con-
cerned with human pain. They're not in actual communi-
cation with any force other than the Dragon. The sword of
Saint George is what inspires their actions.   → ???

Set against these churches is an Islam that forgets all
too often that the divine mercy affirmed by the first verse of
the Koran can only be expressed by human mercy. Their
shared existence is a dry flood whose passage leaves more
cadavers than flowers.

The four young men seated in this classroom are not
merely judges. They are the victims of a very long and very
old tradition of man's capitulation before Destiny. For them,

can't blame them
they are victim of circumstance
come from both sides

65

capital D

NOT GUILTY

the decision of the group is the one thing they must defend and assert by whatever means. They train themselves to become executioners, all the while believing themselves to be judges.

mad for death

They are moved by a sick sexuality, a mad love, where images of crushing and cries dominate. It's not that they are deprived of women or men if they like, but rather are inhibited by a profound distaste for the sexual thing. A sense of the uncleanliness of pleasure torments them and keeps them from ever being satisfied. Thus, the Arabs let themselves go in a tearing, killing, annihilating violence, and while other peoples, virulent in their own obsession with cleanliness, invent chemical products, they seek a primitive and absolute genocide. In their fights they don't try to conquer lands, but to eliminate each other. And if after death they persist in mutilating the corpse, it's to diminish the enemy's body still more, and erase if possible the fact that he ever existed, the existence of the enemy being a kind of sacrilege which exacts a purification equally as monstrous.

They don't feel the opposition between that internal road which leads back to the tribe, and that need that one feels under other skies, to break down the barriers and take a look around, like liberated goats, to go randomly towards a humanity that moves to the rhythm of the turning stars. It's not the first time that an Arab woman has shown such courage before them, but their memories are rebellious. They see greater virtues in their cars than in their women.

66

Marie is strong good

sexist pigs

virulent. (of a disease or poison) extremely severe or harmful in its effect

Their women only exert indirect powers over them, powers that seem ineffective, or else are so strong that they, the men, can't recognize them as such. But a woman who stands up to them and looks them in the eye is a tree to be cut down, and they cut it down. She falls with the sound of dead wood which disappears among the perfidious murmurings of the city, and to the smirking of other women who are satisfied with the male victories.

They only admit to good qualities in their mothers because they remember a well-being in them and around them, which they have never left, even if it were only to go kill birds and other men.

The exclusive love of the mother sets the cycle of violence in motion again. When a stranger appears on the horizon, or the poorly-loved, he is the dispossessed whose hatred sprouts and grows before the eyes like jungle plants that don't even wait for the rain to stop, to proliferate, then he, the one loved by his mother and blessed with wealth, takes his rifle and goes to the attack. He feels he's the strongest, and doesn't know that those bullets will carve bloody words on his naked chest. Deadly, like the stranger, he too will disappear.

How long must we wait for the impossible mutation? It's fear, not love, that generates all actions here. The dog in the street looks at you with terror in his eyes. The combatant has the mentality of a cave man, and despite his courage, goes forward with a mask, or huddles for hours

behind sandbags. Snipers, mercenaries, attracted by the
bad smell of this war, lie in wait for their prey, like snakes.
They are ashamed of their appetite for crime, and odiously
proud of their ability, and yet they hide, in the night of their
veins, a kind of panic that drove them to kill Arabs in
Algiers, blacks in the Congo, and Moslems or Christians in
Beirut. The citizens of this country are accustomed to fear,
fear, the immense fear of not deserving their mother's love,
of not being first at school or in the car race, of not making
love as often as the other guys at the office, of not killing as
many birds as their neighbor, of being less rich than the
Kuwaitis, of being less established in their history than the
Syrians, of not dancing as well as the Latin-Americans, of
being less of a break-neck and extremist than the Palestinian
terrorists.

Marie-Rose frightens them. They have all the means in
the world to crush her in a second, to subject her to all forms
of disgrace; to throw her, cut into pieces, onto the sidewalk,
and register her name on their bulletins of victory. But
they've known from the beginning that they wouldn't be
able to conquer either her heart or her mind. The more she
spoke to them of love, the more they are afraid. Mounir,
Tony, Fouad, and even Bouna Lias, an orphan who had
never known his mother, finding themselves before a woman
who can stand up to them, are terrified. She breaks on the
territory of their imaginations like a tidal wave. She rouses
in their memories the oldest litanies of curses. To them,

love is a kind of cannibalism. 同类相食 Feminine symbols tear at them with their claws. For seven thousand years the goddess Isis has given birth without there being a father. Isis in Egypt, Ishtar in Bagdad, Anat in Marrakesh, the Virgin in Beirut. Nothing survives the passing of these divinities: they 冷眼 only loved Power, their Brother or their Son. And you expect Marie-Rose to hold her head up to this procession of terrible women, and find grace in the eyes of the males of this country?

She thinks of that "other" whom she has just left, and who waits for her with her children in mortal apprehension. She had met him in the narrow streets of the Sabra camp the day she went to the U.N.W.R.R.A. for the first time. She was trying to find her way around, casually looking at the children playing, the multi-colored laundry hung out on lines, the little houses with the colored walls, the old people looking out windows that had neither bars nor glass. He was returning from the dispensary where he had been the doctor on duty that day. She spoke first, in a severe tone as though to insure that he would not think she was being forward. He understood, smiled, responded.

One evening while she was having a lemonade in a café in the Hamra, he was there. He sat down with her and they chatted. He was happy to hear her speak of the Palestinians with such affection. "We need more people like you," he said, "who know that we're not wolves." She laughed. She didn't tell him that she directed an organization that worked for their cause.

A feeling of well-being surrounded the café. Outside, the movie theaters were all in a row. Groups of young people, mostly office workers, salesgirls, students on holiday, male hairdressers, and shirt salesmen passed and repassed, zigzagging through the cars which also loitered there. Everyone moved in slow-motion because no one wanted time to pass.

Suddenly she felt a need to confide in him the discovery of the day, an idea of the kind she hadn't had for very long. On her walk from her house to this café where she was waiting for the box office of the Saroulla Cinema to open for the nine o'clock show, a huge idea had filled her brain: each passing person, she said, is full of his own term of time. Everyone lives Time. If then one added every second lived by each of these people, lived by each of us, by all the people of the world, at this precise moment, it would make all the eternity of Time. She told herself that she had just discovered a new dimension. She had just been thinking these things sipping her lemonade through her straw as he came up and sat down before her.

He had asked her if she was worried about something. She laughed and began to tell him how time was as infinite as space and as mysterious, using her hands to draw invisible lines and spheres. He was a bit stunned, but very amused.

She had gone home happy to have talked to a man

Him listening to her made her feel beautiful

who, though she wore glasses and spoke of serious things, didn't seem bored. She asked herself if she were not perhaps prettier than she had thought.

She saw him again at the funeral of Ghassan Kanafani who was killed starting his car by a bomb designated for him. She walked behind the coffin with the other women dressed in black. He walked tranquilly before, in the group of the militants of the Resistance, their eyes red, their lips tired, their hands open. She saw how haggard these people were, and understood the nature of their new wandering. These were no longer nomads comforted by their tribe and their herd, but a people perpetually pursued, as if by some cosmic agreement, by both an outer and inner enemy, by their self-proclaimed brothers as well as the adversary, without a single square meter of certainty or security under their feet. They would have to forge a nation in the midst of total hostility. They breathed air laced with betrayal.

Marie-Rose and the young doctor found themselves together before the coffin of the assassinated militant poet. Together, they left the little cemetery of exile, in the disorder of the crowd. For a few steps they walked hand in hand, but they became embarrassed and separated. He followed and finally caught up with her, and, as the hot afternoon waned, they walked without a word under a threatening sky, through the streets to the both lively and sad Zarif quarter where she had lived with her children since leaving her husband. The children were absent. They were spending a week of vaca-

71

tion with their paternal aunt. Marie-Rose was alone. So was he. He didn't wait long before taking her in his arms. She didn't protest. During the night he never once said "You are my wife," or "You are the mother of my children." He didn't need to mentally project a pornographic film seen on a trip to Denmark, in order to possess her with pleasure. He simply wanted to be completely with her, and she with him. And when he said to her, "I think I love you," she knew it was true, and there, in the darkness, kept her eyes closed.

The news of her capture had the impact of a submarine missile in the camps. "Allah bring her back," some said, while others said, "Blessed Virgin, we'll light a hundred candles for you if you just send her back to us safe and sound." The young doctor who for months had cared for the wounded seeing some recover and some remain in agony, who had operated sometimes without anesthesia or during power outages by the light of an assistant's flashlight, and who had trained himself to avoid pity in order to hold on, because he knew misfortune had moved in for a long stay, took off for hours from the war and paced around and around in his room. He took the time out to cry. He discarded all that he knew. He forgot his name and his age. He was reduced to nothing but the consciousness of his own pain. He went out into the street, avoiding the eyes of all who knew him, to walk among the garbage cans at the feet of some stunted pines that were even sicker than his patients, and for which he felt a strange affinity. These spindly trees survived with as much difficulty as the Palestinians and they had already seen other bombardments of the refugee camps, other disasters. He said to them, they've captured her and they're going to make her suffer. They're merciless. All the suffering of Palestine was in the muteness of those trees. He felt powerless to help her and strangely humiliated.

He came back to the underground shelter that served as a hospital for a few minutes, before going out again to run to the General Headquarters at the front. The patients were taking advantage of the truce to rest, at least those who were still up to it.

In the various western quarters of the capital, in the sectors allied to the Palestinians, even in families accustomed to tragic news that was repeated with the monotony of weather reports, there rose a kind of death-rattle. Sensibilities, though almost dulled by the daily dose of pain, experienced an enormous shock. Telephone calls became more numerous, people went out into the streets to question each other, stunned, and carried to the point of rage. Everyone knew how horrible this war was, but this woman's capture brought to light a feeling of revolt against the injustice of the war which up until then had been held clenched inside.

Contradictory rumors began to circulate through the city where naturally fertile imaginations had been over-excited for months and months.

While people looked for her all over, and her capture was at first denied by the various suspected parties, and then

confirmed, she was still watching them there seated before
her, still calm enough to detect that the over-charged life
the whole country had been living had gotten to them, cut
them down, and debilitated them like a stiff and apparently
inert muscle. Her own mind was a kind of boat ferrying between the outside world she had unwillingly abandoned
with her loved ones, her friends and her reason for being,
and these four faces that were now the masters in a place
where she was used to being mistress. She was their prisoner
to a complete degree, because for a long time now moral
and judicial law had been suspended, and reason itself had
foundered.

Mounir was a complete stranger to her now. It seemed
to her that she had left the world to which he belonged light
years ago if she had ever actually been a part of it. He wore
his elegant clothes while his comrades wore the party uniform.
Violence had not marked him. Murder, torture—he had
managed to avoid being party to them, and above all, not to
feel responsible for them. He was still the perfect rich kid.
She felt she was being judged by creatures from outer
space. They were completely locked into their own logic.
They were impermeable to everything. She saw in the slight
sea-sickness that had become her thoughts, the sign of the
difference between their world and hers. She carried herself back to the brown faces, the agile bodies, the willfulness
made out of anguish, and the need for survival of the young
Palestinians. Wandering had put questions into their eyes

which, at the moment they felt accepted, quickly became luminous sparks. She needed them. She was suffocating.

Mounir found again vis-à-vis her a complete autonomy. He was hostile towards her. During the two months since he had thrown himself into his clan's battle, he had been constantly irritated. Everything annoyed him that was not directly linked to his new functions. Before his maps and figures, his plans for defending this building, or bombarding that neighborhood, he found a milder tone, a calm, an equilibrium. Away from these things, the old flaws of a spoiled child took the forefront. He was fighting—that was all there was to it. For what? To preserve. To preserve what? His group's power. What was he going to do with this power and this group? Rebuild the country. What country? Here, everything became vague. He lost his footing. Because in this country there were too many factions, too many currents of ideas, too many individual cases for one theory to contain. Like the presence of this woman, taken at random at a roadblock, who should, according to the norms, be a part of his clan, his flesh and blood. He wanted to construct a country where this sort of problem could not exist. But the problem came before the ideal country Mounir wanted to build. He would have to fight the dissident Christians to save the real Christians. His head spun.

But how do you think a judgment could be made in these wretched times? How could Justice remain alive in a country so saturated with covetousness? How could anyone manage to see clearly through so many layers of half-cooked ideas jostling in the myth-stuffed brains which have turned into cages for parrots?

The air that the men who direct the Arab world breathe is particularly wicked. (It is time to call a cat a cat and wickedness an alloy of stupidity and envy.) No one is interested in anything but his own destiny. It's always the destiny of others that must be conquered and destroyed. A true political enterprise, the opposite of oppression, does not exist here. And oppression, God, how they know how to do that. If the human spine could be adapted to it, they would oblige people to walk on all fours. The political enterprise that they don't know is similar to the poetic one. Che Guevara and Badr Chaker el Sayab have this in common that neither of them can be imitated. It is always the next phase, the next poem or the next march through the jungle that shapes them. Our leaders live sitting. When they arrive in power they grow into their chairs, until they, body and chair, become inseparable. In this society where the only freedom of choice, when there is any, is between the different brands of automobiles, can any notion of Justice exist, and can genocide not become an inescapable consequence?

Thus, when the impossible mutation takes place, when, for example, someone like Marie-Rose leaves the normal order of things, the political body releases its antibodies in a blind, automatic process. The cell that contains the desire for liberty is killed, digested, reabsorbed.

- Greed → blind leading blind.
- me against the world
- Individualism   - naive to big picture
                       - Ignorant

* What people in power
  want, to destroy ourselves   III

~ b/c men killing our people
  oppressing own people through false traditions & ideologies

- Sit back and watch us eliminate ourselves

- our only freedom is not impactful very materialistic
- Break free of ignorance to find justice, as long as you
  dwell in these false ideas their will be no Justice,
         [This Ignorance]

1.

deaf-mutes

choose to be ignorant

We're going to the window to look outside. That's always more fun than learning to read on lips things that, most of the time, we'd rather not know, and about which we don't have much to say. But we do have things to say, lots and lots of things, but no one's interested.

It's the second day . . . where did they sleep last night? We went up to our dormitory and this morning they woke us up, made us get into line, and made us come down into the classroom just as usual. Though, this year, school hasn't been what it used to be. There are interruptions, long holidays, classmates who have gone far away to France and England, while we're stuck here, waiting for the war to end. This war has changed the colors of everything we see. Men wear less and less blue. They're grayer. Sometimes they wear military uniforms. The cars have also changed. There are a lot of vans, and jeeps that go very fast. No one seems to be afraid of breaking them. The cats are also freer than before, no one hits them or chases them away. They're on balconies, roofs, walls, sidewalks, garbage cans, demolished buildings. There are a lot of rats all over too. And the cats don't eat them anymore!

There they are still, sitting before us. It's like in the movies. They're very scary. There will be no recess for us today. If it's like yesterday there won't be any recess. But why doesn't she tell them to go away? It's true that there haven't been any policemen for a very long time. Is she afraid of them, she who's never afraid? We look and look at her but her eyes never meet ours. Her eyes say nothing. They're blue like the sky. The sky. Our father the sky.

If only we could be grown-ups all of a sudden. We'd defend her. We'd beat up those guys like Mohammed Ali, the champion. We'd break their heads and twist them right off their necks. But how could we do that now?

Lately, there have been a lot of funerals. Funerals are sad but they're better than going to school. There are always a lot of flowers and it smells good. This year there have been more funerals and less flowers. There have even been people who didn't get buried. No one knows where they are. There have also been fewer weddings, fewer parties than usual. But it's as though there's been a different kind of party. People who can talk and hear must have a lot of fun in war. They look so happy. We are locked in.

We're beginning to get the feeling that something really bad is going to happen. We're tired of waiting. Something really bad is going to happen. Those men are getting more and more ferocious. Their eyes are bloodshot. They look at Sitt Marie-Rose with eyes like cats have in the dark, eyes that do more than just glow. Everything glows. Everything glows. When they were walking around in the street they wore masks cut out of their mothers' stockings, that made them look like pigs or cows. What were they doing that was so bad that they had to hide themselves? But now it's worse. They're even scarier. They quiver. They look like a stormy sky. And we feel hot and cold at the same time.

Sitt Marie-Rose trembles but, with her, everything's always different. We love her so much. More than our parents. More than cakes. More than weekends. More than the sea. If she went away, we'd go too. Where, we don't know, but we'd go away from here.

But she's not going anywhere. Where could she go? There's the war, and there are no boats. They bombed the airport and there are no planes leaving.

She never does anything bad, Sitt Marie-Rose. She's good. She always tells us not to pull dogs' tails, and not to fight in the yard, and not to catch cold when we sweat too much.

These people talk and talk. They're tiring her. They're wearing her out. They're making her suffer. And yet, she's the boss. All she has to do is tell them to go away. But who can she call to help her? And how? There are no more people in this neighborhood.

They've forgotten all about us, but we see everything. One of them has left and the others are all on her. Devils have come up from underground and they've fallen on her. There's an explosion in the air and a return of trees into this room. Everything's spinning. No human being would ever do what they're doing. Where did they come from? How did they get so wild? She's been drowned! She's been drowned! In blood. Perhaps one day speech and sound will be restored to us, we'll be able to hear and speak and say what happened. But it's not certain. Some sicknesses are incurable.

The hope for humanity
the "goodness"

sickness = corruption?

2.

Marie Rose

Why is the light so white this morning? An abrasive pain scrapes at my throat. What do you want of me?

One could say that the city killed itself so that I could dive into the infinity of life before entering the infinity of death. The complicity of heaven is my only recourse now. It's in the dark that the walls close in the most. All through this night I lost track of my ankles, my knees, my stomach, my neck. I lined up numbers in my mind and counted them. I chased fear out of my mind but it impregnated everything. The air thickened and I swallowed it like a ball.

I called prayers to my rescue, but they wouldn't come. Hatred took me in its vice. The muscles of my chest contracted, and the tightness went right up to the nape of my neck like an iron hand. I almost suffocated more than once during this night that seemed to never end. I writhed in a cold sweat and was afraid to cry out, and in their sockets my eyes pained me as though they wanted to abandon me. The thickness of the night could have been cut with a knife. My saliva refused to come and I was exhausted.

What do you want of me? To make me span time as others span rivers? To separate me from this living tree which forms all that I love? I saw little red stars swirling with a deafening sound. I made them be quiet. They returned to scream around the bed that I occupied for certainly the last time. The abyss that lies between the horizontals of sleep and death is the most difficult to cross. I repeated this distance like a child repeats his homework. I learned by heart something that's never taught.

Here I am on a battlefield. It's a terrain closed in on all sides where it is absolutely essential that someone dies. Death always designates the presence of a battle.

To all landscapes there is a particular configuration. The one I'm on is flat, with no grass, just chairs. There are no trees, just a blackboard. There are no horses, only militia men. There are no peasant-witnesses, only handi-capped children. There's no powder, no bombs, just instru-ments of torture.

Death is never in the plural. Let's not exaggerate its victory. It's total enough. Let's not sing about that victory. There are not millions of deaths. It happens millions of times that someone dies.

He's on the other side of town, the one who is waiting for me. He's gnawed by anxiety and weeps. Our comrades are also gnawed by anxiety. We all are whenever one of us is a little late or disappears for too long. Some have never returned. Some have only come back cut into pieces, delivered to their mother's door in plastic bags.

Beirut is a port. Never has any port been so blockaded. Never has a city lived under such an iron sky.

My love had promised me an apple orchard. Today, it's death that's promised me. At this moment I feel closer to him than ever. All night I spoke to him, telling him that I love him, and consoling him for my loss. Did he hear me? His fight must continue. I know it will. For me, the road ends here.

I am weary. My death, after all, will deprive them of very little. It's a beautiful day on the other side of the city, and the streets, even with the bullets flying, are still lively. Oh how innocent and courageous are these people whose vitality defies death! Will the lights shining in their eyes be extinguished one by one? Must a sinister dawn spread like a shroud over their beloved bodies? Must the agility of our young people be crushed by tanks? Must they live and die without their own territory when even a wolf has one? Must this mixture of fear, hate and envy defeat their vigor? If only I could be sure that they would survive my death for a long time!

Where are all the curses for which our race is famous? I haven't the strength for imprecations, nor the desire to imagine new misfortunes. God, whoever you are, protect the future generations from the genocide that awaits them.

Hope

I want to make my peace with everyone. Even with my captors, I want to make my peace. I can no longer sustain this hatred. It's what brought us to this apocalypse.

Chase away the flies buzzing around my head, lift off those weights. I don't want to sleep, to lose the last few hours that are left, these last few minutes while the faces of my loved ones are still familiar in my memory. I don't want to wait for the haggard morning, that passing from hot to cold, and the trembling that takes hold of me. I wouldn't wish that on anyone. I am walled in at the will of my executioners, caught between the finger and the windowpane like a fly. I can no longer stand knowing that I'm about to die. I can't stand it anymore. Can't stand it. I'm already closer to the shadow than to the light.

3.

dialogue

"We've got to hurry. The truce is broken this morning, and we've got to hurry. I've done everything to find you a way out, but you've got to help."

"I have nothing to say to you."

"The enemy camp has made contact to ask us to exchange you for some prisoners, I mean hostages, that they're detaining. They went so far as proposing that they exchange eleven hostages for you alone. One of your chiefs called the Party's Office."

". . . . ."

"You have nothing to say? I've been getting more and more impatient with you, and yet I'm still trying to save your life."

"You can't exchange me. I'm not an object. What makes you think that I wouldn't rather die than serve as the small change in one of your transactions? Even in war you're still nothing but rug merchants."

87

"It'll do you no good to insult us. You have your children. At least you could think of them."

How could I tell my children that I owed my life to such a deal?"

"So you'd prefer to keep your pride?"

"You've understood nothing in all of this. You're fighting like blindmen. You're cutting the throats of innocent people."

"They are and always have been foreigners. They are as out of place here as a fox is in a wolf's den."

"And you want me to give myself up to your sordid bargains?"

"No one said that the terms of this exchange had been accepted. The Party Head Office has already refused. But it will accept the other offer that they're making. Your Palestinian 'friend' offered to make himself our prisoner in your place. He must be a real fanatic to your cause. You've lived together for seven years. That's a long time. He's a significant figure in your hierarchy. It would be a good catch for us. I have advised the Party chiefs to take this offer. It will settle up everyone's accounts. And you will be freed."

You'd dare touch that man? You assassins! You'd fall on him like a pack of hyenas. You'll tear him to pieces and scatter his bones. You assassins! For a year you've been piling up corpses, and now you want to add the body of the man I love. For a year you've been trying to exterminate the Palestinian people. You're nothing but mercenaries. Their bodies have become a part of your soil. You'll inhale them with every breath. You'll eat them in your fruit, drink them from your rivers. You'll find them in your beds and recognize their features in your children. You assassins! I'll tear your eyes out. God, how it hurts!"

Tony

4.

Mounir and I are bound by blood. Normally, I always listen to and follow him, him the water skiing champion and the best hunter, while I'm always second. Now, he's in command. He's the smartest of all of us, but I've proved my courage. He hesitates. He stays in the offices until all the fighting's over, and then he comes out to tally up the dead on both sides. He's never killed anyone with his own hands. Me, I'm braver than a lion. I am, in my own way, a leader of men, like he is. I'm a walking target. The others use my temerity as an example, and the admiration I see in their eyes is my only compensation. The war has leveled our social differences, making us, at last, all equals. Marie-Rose is not indispensable to the legend we're in the process of making. She's just a drop of water from a pond. I could hang her head on my tree of victory. I won't though. Mounir wouldn't accept it. And it doesn't matter that much to me. This hill has remained impenetrable. It's not a kingdom of course, but a den for wild animals. We have complete freedom. No one comes up here. Not a bird. Not a fly. All alone on the summits. Mounir trembles at the sight of human blood. Animal blood doesn't bother him. He'll get used to it. Because this war is going to last a long time. As long as there's a Palestinian living on our land we'll keep fighting. As long as I live, they'll die. I swear it on the cross I wear.

5.

Fouad

The human being is just another cockroach encumbering Nature. This female monster dares stand up to us when she's at our mercy. What a fool! I should have squashed her like a bedbug the moment we captured her. They want to go on talking, questioning her, and for what? Mounir wants to keep his cool. He's crazy. Thousands of deaths should have erased these affectations of false civility. Me, I know that might makes right, that the wolf doesn't ask the sheep's permission to eat him. It's his right as a wolf.

She howled like a dog. She scratched my face. She vomited on my pants. But I quartered her with my own hands. And these imbecile childen watching us. They'll never forget what it costs to be a traitor. The battle is on again. The boom of the cannon, what a sound!

Mens right as rulers of women?

92

Marie Rose & Bouna Lias

6.

dialogue

"My daughter, your time is drawing near. The demon is waiting. The crucifix above your head is suffering. These are no ordinary times. Christianity is in danger. It's no time to be obstinate. The Lord has provided confession so that you can wipe your slate clean. You know that well. All you have to do is sincerely regret the aid you gave to our enemies. You were motivated by a pure heart, I'm sure, but also by an ignorant mind. I'm certain you didn't know how much they wanted to do us evil.

"I myself have defended their cause so often, in religious councils, in sermons on Sunday, in the many little churches on the Mountain. I said that Our Lord's land was occupied and its inhabitants were living miserably in the camps. We were generous. We took them in and then they went to those international crooks, and transformed their camps into dens of thieves. They brought in red Japanese, Pakistani killers. They blaspheme against the name of God, and

93

even go as far as to say that the Almighty does not exist."

"I am exhausted, Bouna Lias. Your words mean nothing to me. You speak mechanically, without knowing what you say. There is no nuance in this country, no shadow. The sky is blue, your eyes are white, and your hearts black. That's how it is. How can I make you back up, make you understand that they're not your enemies, but our brothers, in both flesh and History."

"My daughter, the Chabab are going to make you suffer, and I would like to spare you from their tortures."

"You're worried about me suffering? What about the suffering you imposed on the people for centuries, the suffering you accepted that the people should endure, those generations of humiliation, and all in the name of what? Of whom?"

"You don't expect me to try and explain divine will to you?"

"They said to you, 'Love thy neighbor,' and you eat each other. You plant bombs under Red Cross ambulances because they also treated 'their' wounded. You've forgotten what it means to be human. Hyenas, reptiles, pigs, don't harm their own kind the way you know how to do. And all that in the name of the love of the clan. What am I saying? You're practicing idolatry towards the group you belong to."

"You reject the nobility which binds us together, the devotion our young men show dying for their party, their final act of love for their comrades?"

94

"What love? More than a hundred million Arabs and not one knows how to love! You're only in love with yourselves, you look for your own image in all your attachments, your passion is always directed back on yourselves. No, Bouna Lias, the religious authorities, both Moslem and Christian, have transformed your hearts into deserts, infinitely more arid than the ones we cross on foot in all seasons. I know that the only true love is the love of the Stranger. When you have cut the umbilical cords that bind you together, you will at last become real men, and life among you will have a meaning."

"May God pardon you, my daughter. You have no feeling for the beauty of this country, for the days still before you, for your own youth."

"This country is stained with blood. The walls are spattered with blood, and there is not a single child who has not seen with his own eyes either a corpse or an execution. It's a sick world, a whirlpool, with oil in its cisterns, and cannons on the terraces of its monasteries."

"We're going to rebuild it, and try to forget. . . ."

"Rebuild what? A city with no soul, no pity? New banks and new slums. You'll start polluting the water again, the fields, the streets, and people's minds. You want me to survive? To do what? To live where?"

"If you don't care about your body, at least think of your soul."

"What gives you the right to pretend you can save

souls? When you sow hate, you sow evil without redemption. No! You have also perverted Christ. No! You emasculated the students in your schools and universities, making them submit to your will, humiliating them hour after hour, until finally, in order to reaffirm themselves they found murder was their only recourse. In order to escape your influence, but without being conscious of it, they do your dirty work."

"You know nothing of the resurrection that awaits them. We have put this war under the sign not of politics but of the divine. In this century no one has fought with holy medals on as many chests, the Virgin on as many rifles, the crucifix on as many tanks, the name of God on so many lips, the vision of Heaven before so many eyes, as our young men. It's an army of saints on the march, who pay with their lives for the sins of a humanity that never stops crucifying Christ."

"Yes, you've made them insensible to pain by glorifying thorns and nails, glorifying blood as a beverage and human flesh as nourishment. They exalt themselves with flagellation, and passed their childhoods hearing terrifying stories of Hell. In your schools that smell of incense and sweat they identified with Christ and the executioner, taking themselves first for the one and then for the other. They kill and mutilate with a rosary in their hands, believing that they serve the Virgin. And you want me to bow before such a fantasy?"

"Your soul is going to sink Marie-Rose, you who bear the name of both the Virgin and her symbol. Families will speak of you and your treason for a long time to come, and without mercy."

"If I had to say what families are! Hardened muscle, blocked horizons, caldrons where evil stews, oppressive cells. They are also your victims. You taught them that the ideal family consists of a Christ without a father, and a mother who like the Arab woman loves no one but her son."

"Stop, Marie-Rose. You're depraved and sacrilegious. You're swimming in madness.

"Yes, Lord, Thy will be done. I tried to bring back one of Thy own and she resisted. The cries I hear now are the sign of the punishment Thou has sent from Heaven. These young men are executing Thy Providence. They leave nothing on the ground but a pile of dislocated members that was a sinner. I can give her neither extreme unction nor benediction. She no longer has a face. She has fallen before Thy Judgment. She is Thy responsibility. She will no longer be ours. On this earth we defend Thy interests, and those of Thy Beloved Son, so that Thy will be done, on Earth as it is in Heaven, and the keys to the Great Mystery stay in Thy hands alone. Amen."

7.

Omniscient
problematic

Final

Keep them separate ↗ man/machine

I want to talk about the light on this day. An execution always lasts a long time. I want to say forever and ever that the sea is beautiful, even more so since the blood washed down by the greedy rain opened reddening roads into the sea. It's only in it, in its immemorial blue, that the blood of all is finally mixed. They have separated the bodies, they have separated the minds, those who govern as well as those foreigners brought on a wind from the West, those from Iran and the Soviet Union, all, all have sown poison herbs in these peasant mentalities, in these uprooted brains, in these slum children, in their schizophrenic student logic. They have done this so that the population, turning a hundred ways at once, loses its way, and sees every mobile being as a target or a sure threat of death. Madness is like a hurricane, and its motion is circular. It all turns around and around, drawing circles of fire in this country, which has become nothing but a closed arena, and in this city which is nothing but a huge square of cement. They circle around each other in their hollow arguments, hollow like their ramshackle walls, their hatred, their blindness. They only address each other with cannons, machine guns, razors, knives. And the sea, receiving them in an advanced state of decomposition, reconciles them in the void.

What is the light like on a day of execution? An ordinary light. It's only in our heads that electric light bulbs spin and the heat of the day explodes. It's our heads that irradiate and change Nature. It's because they still function with the momentary independence of machines, that one asks oneself how behind their windows, behind their piece of wall, people still survive, women alone, women and men, men alone, etc. Why don't animals come and rent houses, or why isn't there a coming and going of Martians, moonmen, spacemen, a new animation on this ravaged landscape? Why is everything so ordinary?

When I'm right I know it. The temperature of my hands rises to let me know. Something quakes through my body. Everything becomes silent around me and I see it. The silence makes a sort of halo. My head becomes an empty water-skin without resonance, the inner lining clean and stretched. Everything freezes. There's a slight buzzing like the sound the earth makes turning in space. I'm right, oh, how right I am! Then I take off, believing that I'm really free of the cage. But to discover a truth is to discover a fundamental limit, a kind of inner wall to the mind, so I fall again to the ground of passing time, and discover that it's Marie-Rose who's right.

It must be said, said so that this civilization that was born in the night of time, and now finds itself dazed before the nuclear wall, brought to its knees before this new Power, hears what its masses want to tell it, so that it can scale the final mountain. Like patients maintained with transfusions of blood and food, the Arab world lies on an operating table. The equipment should be removed, the respirator unplugged. The patient should be obliged to spit out, not the mucous, but the original illness, not the blood clogging his throat but the words, the words, the swamp of words that have been waiting there for so long.

Look at them! Those four men set upon that passing bird. They bend over her case with the posture of rug merchants, and the age-long heavy gestures of connoisseurs of merchandise. She was, they admit, a worthy prey, though they don't consider her a museum piece, real booty, an exemplary catch. She was a woman, an imprudent woman, gone over to the enemy and mixing in politics, which is normally their personal hunting ground. They, the Chabab, had to bring women back to order, in this Orient, at once nomadic and immobile. On the Palestinian side, they dealt with crimes similarly. The stakes were different, but the methods were the same.

She made the mistake of venturing into their territory. She overlooked the instinct of the jackal that lies in wait for

100

chickens, that instinct which still exists under the skins of men living from the Gulf to the Atlantic. The scouts of the clan hunt and bring the prey back to the fold. This is a common good, be it in Islamic tribes in southern Tunisia, or in Christian tribes from the Lebanese mountains: the trapped gazelle is always shared by all. In concrete houses or under black tents, they wait for the raiders' return with the eyes and claws of falcons. Every day they nonchalantly trap and take away their quarry, and add another victim's name to their already long list of acts of glory.

She was also subject to another great delusion believing that women were protected from repression, and that the leaders considered political fights to be strictly between males. In fact, with women's greater access to certain powers, they began to watch them more closely, and perhaps with even greater hostility. Every feminine act, even charitable and seemingly unpolitical ones, were regarded as a rebellion in this world where women had always played servile roles. Marie-Rose inspired scorn and hate long before the fateful day of her arrest.

However, fear of torture often crossed her mind. She had told her friends that if she refused to join certain clandestine political parties it was because of her fear of prison. But she supported the Resistance with a profound conviction, and because it seemed more a question of love than politics, a question of Life and Death for all Arabs. She believed that this cause must be sacred to all, and when she suspected hypocrisy, she silenced her mistrust.

Torture preoccupied her because she saw in it, or rather in the person who could resist it, the summit of human courage. She hated physical suffering, abhorred it, and considered it a fundamental injustice to Nature. She was persuaded that men could be cured of moral and physical ills if only, if only. . . . She sometimes managed to convince herself that torture did not exist, while she knew that it was practiced in all the capitals of the world.

One afternoon on the balcony of a friend's house overlooking the city's sole public garden, the one she called the Big Garden in childhood, she met a Belgian journalist, passing through Beirut on his way home from Viet Nam. He had been captured near Saigon by the Viet Cong, and after finally managing to prove his identity, was released after several days. She asked him if he wasn't afraid, and he said that of course he was afraid, he was constantly afraid in Viet Nam. He had decided, in order to overcome his fear, that if he were taken prisoner, or rather if he found himself on the point of being tortured, he would swallow his tongue and try to choke himself to death. He also decided, he said, that if things "got bad" and he could find no way to escape, he would throw such outrageous defiance in the face of his interrogators, that they would speed up their work.

This conversation came back to her very often over the next few years when, in Bagdad, Amman, Damascus, and Jerusalem, nightmares were accumulating. In the streets near these cities' prisons, you could hear the wails of political prisoners. At least, Marie-Rose (as many others) said to herself, people in Lebanon live under regimes that, while corrupt, are still made of "nice guys." No one seemed to want to admit that cruelty was a part of a moral cancer that was spreading through the whole of the Middle East. That was how Beirut became a huge open wound. If suffering could be measured in ounces and square centimeters, then the suffering of this city was greater than any other city in the century. Berlin, Saigon, Madrid, Athens, none of them knew the murder and sadism this city did. Thus, in the smoking bath of acid, under bullets, rockets, napalm and phosphorus bombs, with assassinations and abductions, each being met his personal, definitive apocalypse. Like a bird flying alone in a seemingly untroubled sky, Marie-Rose was cut down by hunters on the look-out.

One still remembers the famous picture drawn by Gamal Abdel Nasser of concentric circles, with Egypt, the Islamic Third World, the rest of the Third World. . . . But this hero of Arab History should have denounced the concentric circles of oppression, and taken on the task of breaking them.

At the center is the individual surrounded by the circle of his family. Then comes the circle of the state, then the circle of the Brother Arab countries, the circle of the Enemy, the Super Powers, and so forth. . . . These circles of oppression are inevitably circles of betrayal. In their interior spaces, lively forces are crushed, annihilated, and apparent confusion is maintained through a mortal order.

Power is always obscene. It's only in thickening the sensibility that the human brain attains power and maintains it, and all power finally expresses itself through the death penalty. Marie-Rose was a blade of grass in the bulldozer's path. The Palestinians too. And the Syrian bulldozers come to take over from the executors of the universal Power. From the east to the Mediterranean, tanks come to continue the work of crushing Life. The circles of oppression have also become circles of repression. Marie-Rose is not alone in her death. Second by second the inhabitants of this city that were her comrades fall. Where the tanks stop, planes take over. Airplanes have become the flies of the Arab world, conceived in a frenzy of power, and the plague they carry is the vehicle of its new curse.

In the classroom, held in their bewildering simplicity, is the group of justices, Mounir, Tony, Fouad, and Bouna Lias. Before them, Marie-Rose, beneath the extinguished electric light bulb hung by a cord, and the deaf-mutes. On the wall there is a crucifix. But, in this room, Christ is a tribal prince. He leads to nothing but ruin. One is never right to invoke him in such circumstances, because the true Christ only exists when one stands up to one's own brothers to defend the Stranger. Only then does Christ embody innocence.

Whether you like it or not, an execution is always a

celebration. It is the dance of Signs and their stabilization in Death. It is the swift flight of silence without pardon. It is the explosion of absolute darkness among us. What can one do in this black Feast but dance? The deaf-mutes rise, and moved by the rhythm of falling bombs their bodies receive from the trembling earth, they begin to dance.

· there is still torture existing today
· injustice

Printed in
the United States of America